For my mom, who encouraged me to grow
—Alison

For Emma, Kate, and Julianna
—Paige

Text Copyright © 2009 Alison Barber
Illustration Copyright © 2009 Paige Keiser

Sleeping Bear Press™

310 North Main Street, Suite 300, Chelsea, MI 48118
www.sleepingbearpress.com

© 2009 Sleeping Bear Press is an imprint of Gale, a part of Cengage Learning.

Printed and bound in China.

10 9 8 7 6 5 4 3 2 1

Library of Congress Cataloging-in-Publication Data
Barber, Alison.
The little green pea / written by Alison Barber ; illustrated by Paige Keiser. -- 1st ed.
p. cm.
Summary: A tiny pea, scorned by the other peas because he dreams of growing into a tree, begins to lose hope
when he is picked to be part of a tuna casserole, but fate and a helpful worm come to the rescue.
ISBN 978-1-58536-448-0
[1. Peas--Fiction. 2. Worms--Fiction. 3. Hope--Fiction.] I. Keiser,
Paige, ill. II. Title.
PZ7.B2318Lit 2009
[E]--dc22
2008040955

The Little Green Pea

Alison Barber

Illustrated by Paige Keiser

In a field among fields, off Interstate 3,
in a patch past the peppers, in row fifty-three,
grew one, little green pea.

But this is no ordinary pea.

This little green pea dreamed night and day
of becoming a tree.

"Hee ha" laughed all of the peas in row fifty-three,

and for that matter too, laughed row fifty-two.

"Use your pea-brain," they cried

"you're too wee to become a tree!"

But this little green pea said,
"No. I'm going to grow!"

And so he soaked up the sun
and drank up the rain,
and he grew... what seemed
an inch or two!

Then one day (hooray!) a guy in galoshes came by.
And he mucked through the mud,
and he plucked and he chucked
the little (not so wee) green pea, along with row fifty-three,
and for that matter too, he shucked row fifty-two
into a rusty blue bucket.

"You see" whispered the little (not so wee) green pea

"This is it! I'm on my way to becoming a tree!"

whee!

hee hee.

"Uh-oh," said the little green pea in a voice very wee

"Is this where I'm supposed to grow? Um- Excuse me-..."

"Dear me," exclaimed the pea,

"do they plan to eat me?"

So he worked up his might to put up a fight,
but with all of the drama to avoid such trauma,
he fell to the floor and rolled out of sight.

"How could this be?" thought the little green pea, "I wanted so much to become a tree. I dreamed night and day, I soaked up the sun and drank up the rain, but is this where I will always remain?"

And the little green pea went all wrinkly.

And then... I ate him up!

Oh, hi. I'm a squirmy worm.

And I've been telling the story all along.

And I especially love wrinkly peas!

So I came along and ate the little green pea up off the floor

and then wiggled out the door...

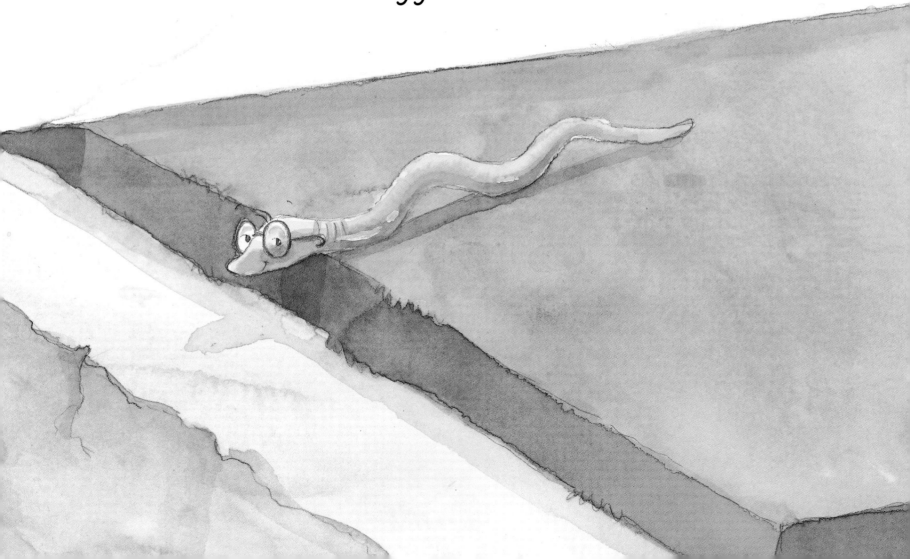

into the yard (it took a while)

but I finally made it back to my mud pile.

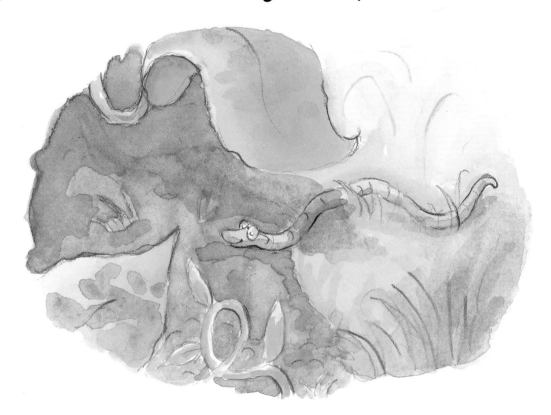

Do not be sad for the little green pea and certainly don't get mad at me! You see, a pea is a seed and wherever they're spat, they mix and

they mingle with this and with that.
We worms do the mixing, the seeds do the mingling
and all of us wiggle and all the while giggle...

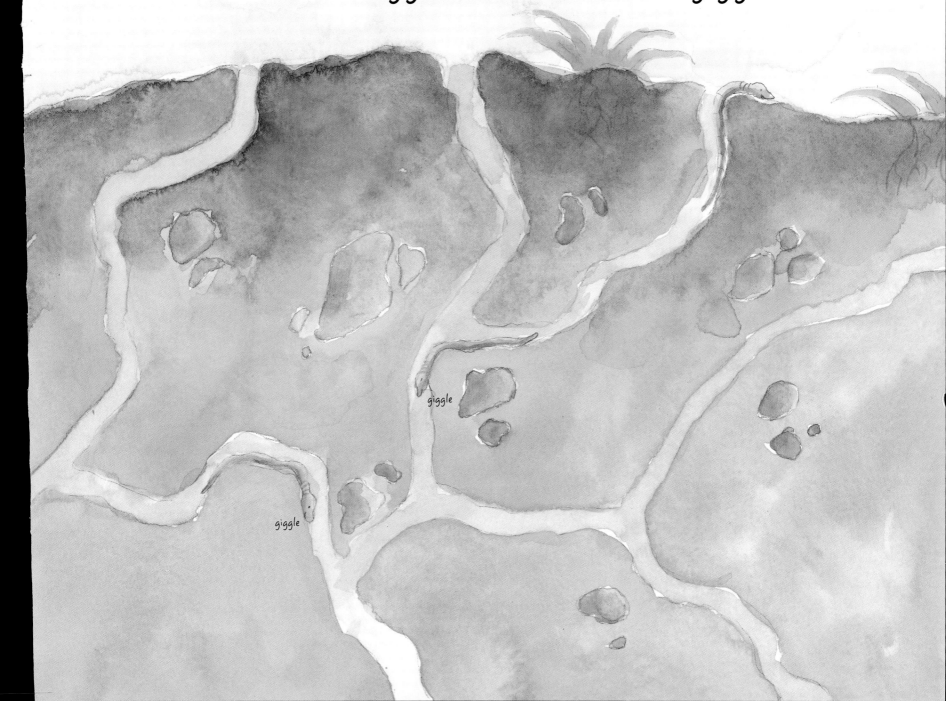

We especially like poo (we really do!)

'cause out of it all, something grew, grew, grew...

hee hee.